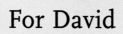
For David

Potty!

Mylo Freeman

TRICYCLE PRESS

Berkeley • Toronto

Near a small village in the middle of a jungle
sits a potty. Beside it is a note that says
"Only the best bottom of all will fit on this potty."

As Zebra passes by, he reads the note and thinks, "My bottom is the best." But Zebra's bottom is much too big.

Next, Giraffe wants to have a try.

"Bend your knees more, or you'll fall over!" calls Zebra.

"Leopard's bottom won't fit either," giggles Giraffe.

"Why don't you tell him?" asks Zebra.

"Oh no, you tell him," says Giraffe.

"Snake looks like he could use a hand,"
says Leopard.

"Ssstay ssstill for a sssecond," Snake hisses
at the potty.

"Elephant is sitting down, but I can't see the potty anywhere," says Zebra.

"Oops! I missed," Elephant tells them.

"Does it fit me?" asks Gorilla.

"Not on your head, silly," the animals call out.

"Just joking!" Gorilla says.

"Let's go have something to eat," says Elephant.
"Tortoise can take a while."

When the animals return, they can't
believe their eyes.

"Who is that?" asks Gorilla.

"He fits on the potty," Tortoise whispers.

"It's so small, that bottom," says Elephant.

"And it has no stripes," says Zebra.

"Or spots," says Giraffe.

"Where is its fur?" wonders Leopard.

"He hasss gone pee-pee in the potty," says Snake.

"That's the best bottom of all!" shouts Tortoise.

And they all agree.

Does your bottom fit on the potty?

First published in 1997 under the title *Potje!*
Copyright © Uitgeverij J.H. Gottmer/H.J.W. Becht BV Haarlem, the Netherlands.
English edition copyright © 2002 by Mylo Freeman
www.mylofreeman.com

Tricycle Press
a little division of Ten Speed Press
P.O. Box 7123
Berkeley, California 94707
www.tenspeed.com

Typeset in Scala

Library of Congress Cataloging-in-Publication Data
Freeman, Mylo.
  [Potje. English]
  Potty! / Mylo Freeman.
      p. cm.
Summary: In the jungle sits a potty with the words, "Only the best
bottom will fit on this potty," which prompts different animals to give
it a try until a stranger shows them who fits it best.
  ISBN 1-58246-070-1
  [1. Toilets—Fiction. 2. Jungle animals—Fiction.] I. Title.
PZ7.F8755 Po 2002
[E]—dc21
                                    2001005188

First Tricycle Press printing, 2002
Printed in Singapore

1 2 3 4 5 6 – 06 05 04 03 02

Leaping Learners
Education, LLC

For more information and resources visit us at:
www.leapinglearnersed.com

ISBN
978-1-948569-19-4

Dear Parents and Guardians,

Thank you for purchasing a *Matt Learns About* series book! After teaching students from kindergarten to second grade for more than seven years, I became frustrated by the lack of engaging books my students could read independently. To help my students engage with nonfiction topics, my wife and I decided to write nonfiction books for children. We hope to inspire young children to learn about the natural world.

Here at Leaping Learners Education, LLC, we have three main goals:

1. Spark young readers' curiosity about the natural world
2. Develop critical independent reading skills at an early age
3. Develop reading comprehension skills before and after reading

We hope your child enjoys learning with Matt. If you or your children are interested in a topic we have not written about yet, send us an email with your topic, and maybe your book will be next!

Thank you,

Sean Bulger, Ed.M

www.leapinglearnersed.com

Reading Suggestions:

Before reading this book, encourage your children to do a "picture walk," where they skim through the book and look at the pictures to help them think about what they already know about the topic. Thinking about what they already know helps children get excited about learning more facts and begin reading with some confidence.

Preview any new vocabulary words with your child. Key vocabulary words are found on the last few pages of the book. Have your children use each new phrase in their own words to see if they understand the definition.

After previewing the book, encourage your child to read the book independently more than once. After they have read it, ask them specific questions related to the information in the book. Encourage them to go back and reread the relevant section in the book to retrieve the answer in case they forgot the facts.

Finally, see if your child can complete the reading comprehension exercises at the end of the book to strengthen their understanding of the topic!

This book is best for ages 6-8
but. . .
Please be mindful that reading levels are a guide and vary depending on a child's skills and needs.

Matt Learns About . . . Toucans

Written by Sean and Anicia Bulger

Table of Contents

Hi! My name is Matt. I love to discover and learn new things. In this book, we will learn about toucans. Let's go!

Introduction

What's a colorful bird that lives in the rainforest?

PG 2

Tricky word:
say
To-can

A toucan!

PG 3

PG 4

Habitat

Where do toucans live?

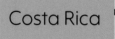

Toucans live in Costa Rica and the Amazon rainforest.

Costa Rica

Amazon

SOUTH AMERIC

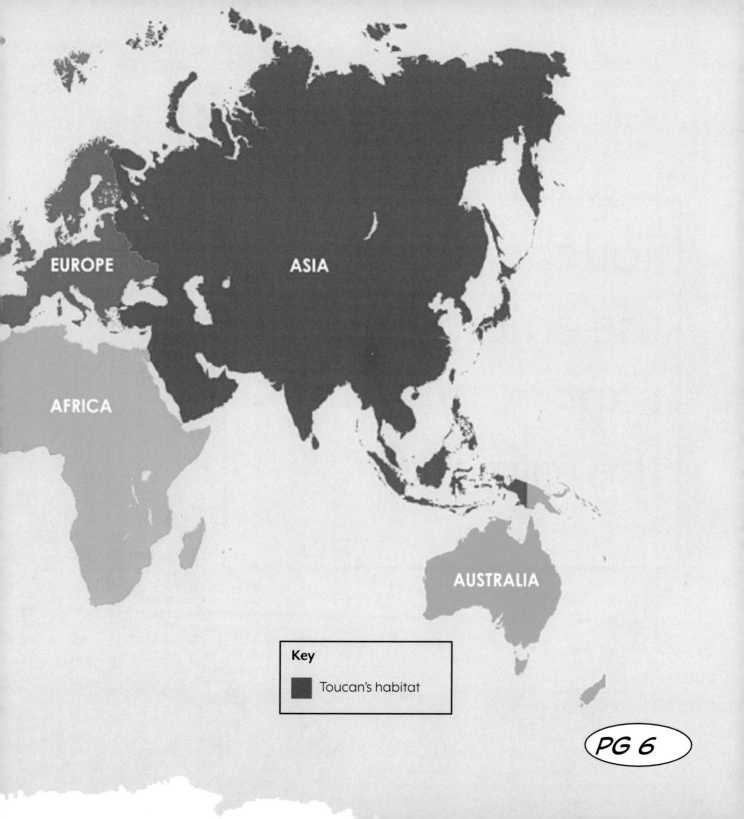

EUROPE

ASIA

AFRICA

AUSTRALIA

Key

Toucan's habitat

PG 6

Toucans live in the emergent and canopy layers of the rainforest.

PG 7

Tricky words: say E-mer-gent and can-o-pee

Toucans make their homes in **hollow** parts of trees.

Hollow

PG 10

<u>Body</u>

What do toucans look like?

Toucans have wings. Toucans fly and hop around branches in the canopy and emergent layers.

The emergent and canopy layers are the two highest layers of the rainforest.

As you can see, toucans have a large, colorful **beak**.

Beak

PG 14

A toucan's beak has **jagged** edges to help it eat.

Jagged

Food

A toucan's favorite foods are fruits, but they also eat insects, eggs, and even other small birds.

What do toucans eat?

Fruit

Toucans use their large beaks to eat their food.

PG 18

Predators

Boa

Which animals eat toucans?

Harpy eagles, boa constrictors, and jaguars are some animals that eat toucans.

Jaguar

Harpy Eagle

PG 20

Staying Safe

How do toucans stay safe?

Toucans stay safe by making loud noises if a predator is near. They will also attack a predator with their beak.

PG 21

Baby Toucans

Where are baby toucans born?

Female toucans lay eggs in the hollow parts of trees. The baby **hatches** from the egg.

Egg

Caterpillar

As a toucan grows up, it likes to eat worms and small insects.

Worm

PG 26

Toucans In Danger

The toucans' natural home is under threat because people are cutting down rainforests and **capturing** toucans to sell as pets.

PG 28

Toucans have one of the largest beak of all birds.

A toucan's beak is made from keratin, which is the same thing our fingernails are made of.

Both male and female toucans sit on their eggs to keep them warm.

Glossary

A glossary tells the reader the meaning of important words.

Hollow – A hole or opening in a tree

Beak – The front part of a bird's mouth

Jagged – Rough or sharp

Hatches – When a baby is born by breaking out of the egg

Capture – To catch or trap something

Draw a picture of a toucan

PG 31

Draw a picture of a toucan eating

The toucan is eating a _____.

Quiz

1. Where do toucans live?

a. In hollow parts of trees

b. Under ground

c. In caves

2. What is one word you can use to describe a toucan's beak?

a. Small

b. Jagged

c. Grey

3. In which section do you learn about the sounds a toucan makes?

a. Staying safe

b. Bodies

c. Food

Common core standards:
RI. 1. 1 - Questions 1, 2
RI. 1. 2 - Question 3

4. What is one thing toucans eat?

a. Anteaters

b. Leaves

c. Fruit

5. What is one animal that eats toucans?

a. Ants

b. Monkeys

c. Jaguars

6. What does the picture on page 16 teach you?

a. What a toucan's beak looks like

b. How toucans fly

c. What animals eat a toucan

Common core standards:
RI. 1. 1 - Questions 4, 5
RI. 1.8 - Question 6

want to learn about ocean animals? Check out the "Fay Learns About..." series!

Great for emerging readers ages 6-8

Want to learn about Farm Animals? Check out the "Katie Teaches you About..." Series!

Great for early readers ages 4-6

Want to learn about colors? Check out the "Clayton Teaches You About..." series!

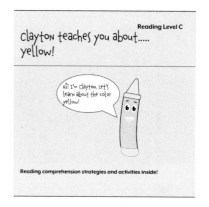

Great for early readers ages 4-6

Made in the USA
Columbia, SC
05 March 2023